You Are Mine

ILLUSTRATIONS BY SERGIO MARTINEZ

MAX LUCADO

CROSSWAY BOOKS · WHEATON, ILLINOIS

A DIVISION OF GOOD NEWS PUBLISHERS

You Are Mine

Text copyright © 2001 by Max Lucado

Illustrations © 2001 by Sergio Martinez

Published by Crossway Books

        a division of Good News Publishers

        1300 Crescent Street

        Wheaton, Illinois 60187

Edited by Karen Hill

Illustrations by Sergio Martinez

Cover design: Uttley/DouPonce DesignWorks (www.uddesignworks.com)

First printing 2001

Printed in the United States of America

ISBN 1-58134-276-4

LIBRARY OF CONGRESS CATALOGING-IN-PUBLICATION DATA

Lucado, Max.
You are mine / Max Lucado; illustrations by Sergio Martinez.
   p. cm.
   Summary: When Punchinello tries to prove his worth by getting more boxes and balls than the other Wemmicks, he learns that his maker, Eli, loves him because of who he is and not what he possesses.
   ISBN 1-58134-276-4 (hc : alk. paper)
   [1. Conduct of life--Fiction.   2. Self-acceptance--Fiction.
   1.Martinez, Sergio, 1937-   . ill II. Title.
PZ7.L9684   Ym 2001
[E]--dc21   2001000235

10   09   08   07   06   05   04   03   02   01

15 14 13 12 11 10 9 8 7 6 5 4 3 2 1

For Royce and Rube Carrigan

God could not love you more than he already does.

PUNCHINELLO LIVED IN Wemmicksville. Just like other Wemmicks, he was made of wood. Just like the other Wemmicks, he was carved by Eli, the Wemmick-maker. And just like the other Wemmicks, he sometimes did silly things. Like the time he began collecting boxes and balls.

Things started getting crazy when a Wemmick named Tuck bought a new box. Others had boxes, but Tuck's was a new box.

Tuck loved his new box. He thought it was the best box in the village. It was brightly colored, and he was proud of it—too proud perhaps. He strutted up and down the street showing off his box.

"Have you seen my new box?" he would ask the Wemmicks he passed on the street. "Would you like to touch my new box?"

Tuck marched right up to Punchinello: "Don't you wish you had a new box?" he teased.

Punchinello thought Tuck's box was beautiful, and he began to wish for a box of his own.

Tuck kept showing off his box, thinking he was better than the other Wemmicks just because he had a new box.

Nip, another Wemmick, disagreed. "My box is just as good as Tuck's," he said, as he showed off his box to Wemmicks on the other side of the street. Nip's box was not new, but it was a bit bigger and a bit brighter and—a bit more than Tuck could take.

Tuck got very quiet and gave Nip a mad look. Then he had an idea. He stepped into a store and bought a ball. Now he had more things than Nip. He had a box and a ball.

Nip frowned at Tuck's ball. Nip could do better than that. He bought two balls. With a smile on his face, two balls and a box in his hands, he marched over to Tuck and smirked, "Now I have more than you!"

Before he knew it, Tuck was in the store buying another box. Then Nip ran to buy another ball. Then Tuck bought a ball, and Nip bought a box.

Ball. Box. Ball. Box.

Tuck. Nip. Nip. Tuck. On and on it went.

Someone could have stopped the whole mess right there. In fact, that's what the mayor tried to do. "You two are being silly," he said to Nip and Tuck, "Why, who cares who has the most toys?"

"You're just jealous," they replied, "because you don't have any."

"Jealous? Of you? Ha!" But within a few moments the mayor was in the store buying an armful of boxes and balls.

Other Wemmicks began to join in. The butcher. The baker. The cabinetmaker. The doctor from up the street and the dentist from down the street. Before long every Wemmick wanted to be the one with the most balls and boxes.

Some boxes were big, and some were bright. Some balls were heavy, and some were light. Tall people carried them. Small people carried them. Everybody carried them. And everybody thought the same thought: *Good Wemmicks have a lot. Not-so-good Wemmicks have little.*

When a Wemmick walked down the center of Wemmicksville with a stack of balls and boxes higher than his head, the people stopped. "Now there goes a good Wemmick," they would say. But when a Wemmick passed by with only one ball or one box, the others would shake their heads and think, maybe even whisper, "Poor Wemmick. Poor, poor Wemmick."

Of course, Punchinello didn't want to be called a poor Wemmick, so he decided to get as many boxes and balls as he could. He searched through his closet and found one little ball. He dug into his pocket and found enough money for one small box.

"I know what I'll do," he declared. "I'll sell my books to get more money to buy more boxes and balls."

So he did. He bought a blue and green box with clouds painted on the sides. But still he wanted more. "I'll work nights to get extra money," he told himself. So he did, and bought a ball. And since he was working nights, he didn't need his bed, so he decided, "I'll sell my bed." And he did just that— to buy two more balls.

Soon Punchinello had an armful. But other Wemmicks had more. Some of them had so many boxes and balls, they actually had trouble walking. "It's hard keeping up with all my balls and boxes," they would say, acting like they were complaining, but really they were bragging.

Punchinello wanted to be like these Wemmicks, so he sold more stuff, and he worked more hours. His eyes were tired from not getting any sleep. His arms were tired from carrying toys. He couldn't remember when he last sat down to rest. And, worst of all, his friends couldn't remember when Punchinello last came to play.

"We haven't seen you for a long time," his friend Lucia said to him one day.

"Why don't you come and play again?" asked his buddy Splint.

Not everyone cared about boxes and balls. Punchinello's friends didn't. But Punchinello cared more about having boxes and balls than he cared about having friends.

"I've got work to do," he would tell them. And his friends would sigh.

Punchinello didn't care. He only cared what the other box-and-ball people thought. And no matter what he did, he couldn't buy enough things to get their attention.

Finally he had an idea. "I will sell my house," he decided.

"That's crazy," cried Lucia.

"Where will you live?" asked Splint.

Punchinello didn't know, but he didn't care. All he could think about was the boxes and balls he would have with all that money. So he sold his house. He bought boxes and boxes and boxes and balls and balls and more balls. He carried so many toys, he couldn't see where he was going. His stack went way above his head.

But he didn't mind. So what if his arms ached? So what if he kept walking into walls? So what if he had no friends? He had boxes and balls, and when he passed Wemmicks, they would turn and say, "Wow, he must be a good Wemmick." Punchinello heard them. He couldn't see them, but he heard them, and he felt good. *I'm a good Wemmick,* he thought.

But then somebody changed the rules. It was the mayor's wife. She was very proud of her boxes and balls. She not only had a lot of them, but she also had special kinds of them. She bought them at the fanciest stores with funny names and left the names on the boxes so everyone would see them. She wanted to be the best Wemmick.

One day she had an idea. "Not only will I have the most, but I will go the highest."

So she climbed on top of one of her boxes and shouted, "Look at me, everybody!"

Immediately all of the box-and-ball people tried to outdo her. One climbed on a fountain, another on a balcony, and then another onto a roof. It was the mayor who spotted the mountain, however.

Behind the village of the Wemmicks was Wemmicks' Peak. "I'm going to the top of the mountain," he shouted, hoping to get there first. The race was on to see which Wemmick would have the most and climb the highest. Wemmicks loaded with boxes and balls began running up the mountain.

It was a crazy, crazy race. Since the wooden people couldn't see where they were going, they bumped into each other. Since they were exhausted, they fell over their own feet. Since the trail was narrow, some fell down the side of it. But they kept going.

Bringing up the rear was Punchinello. He was having a hard climb, harder than the rest. After all, he'd only been a "good Wemmick" for a short time. He wasn't used to carrying so many boxes and balls. But he was determined. He kept putting one little wooden foot ahead of the other. But since he couldn't see, he didn't know he was on the side of the trail.

And since he couldn't see, he didn't know that he had left the trail. All he knew was that—all of a sudden—he was all alone. *I must be ahead of everyone else!* he thought to himself. And so he kept climbing up and up and up. *I must be very near the top. I'm such a good Wemmick; I'll be the highest with the most.*

About that time Punchinello's foot caught the edge of something. He tried to keep his balance—his toys swayed to the right and then to the left. He leaned back, then forward, but he couldn't stop. He was going to fall. He didn't know, however, that he had walked up the trail to Eli's house. He tripped on the step of the porch and tumbled through the front door of Eli's workshop.

When Punchinello realized where he was, he was embarrassed. For a long time he stayed facedown on the floor, surrounded by his boxes and balls. One of the balls rolled across the floor and stopped at Eli's workbench. That's when the woodcarver turned around.

"Punchinello." Eli's voice was calm and deep and kind.

The Wemmick still didn't move. He could feel his wooden face turning red.

"Looks like you've been carrying a big load."

The weary Wemmick climbed to his knees but kept his head low.

"These are my boxes and balls," he said quietly.

"Do you play with the boxes and balls?" asked Eli.

Punchinello shook his head.

"Do you like boxes and balls?"

"I like the way they make me feel."

"And how do they make you feel?"

"Important," Punchinello answered, still with a small voice.

"Hmmm," Eli observed, "so you've been thinking like the other Wemmicks. You've been thinking that the more you have, the better you are, and the happier you'll be."

"I suppose so."

"Come here, Punchinello. I want to show you something."

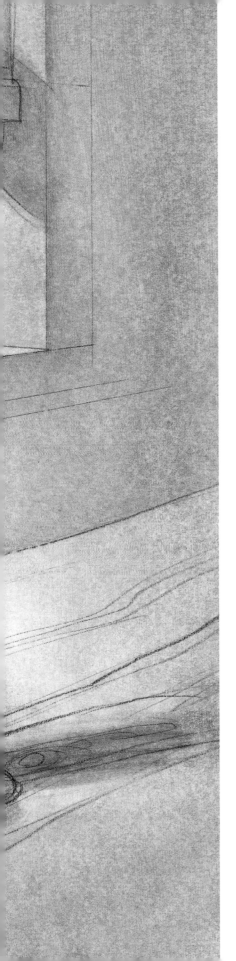

Punchinello lifted his wooden head and looked at Eli for the first time. He was relieved to see that the Wemmick-maker wasn't angry. Punchinello followed Eli over to the window.

"Look at them," Eli said.

Punchinello looked out the window at the swarm of Wemmicks still climbing the mountain. They were tumbling, stumbling, fighting each other, even elbowing each other to get ahead.

"Do they look happy?" Eli asked.

Punchinello just shook his head.

"Do they look important?"

"Not at all," Punchinello said, noticing the mayor and his wife. The mayor was on the ground, and she was stepping on his back. She had a box on her head, and he had a ball in his mouth.

"Do you think I created Wemmicks to act that way?" asked Eli.

"No."

Punchinello felt a big hand on his shoulder. "Do you know how much your boxes and balls cost you?"

"My books and bed. My money and my house."

"My little friend, they cost you much more than that."

Punchinello was trying to remember what else he had sold when Eli continued, "They cost you happiness. You haven't been happy, have you?"

Punchinello paused. "No."

"They cost you friends. And most of all, they cost you trust. You didn't trust me to make you happy. You trusted these boxes and balls."

Punchinello looked at the pile of toys. All of a sudden they didn't seem so valuable.

"I kind of messed up."

"That's okay," Eli replied. "You're still special."

Punchinello ducked his head and smiled.

"You're special—not because of what you have. You're special because of who you are. You are mine. I love you. Don't forget that, little friend."

"I won't." Punchinello smiled. Then he paused and asked, "Eli?"

"Yes."

"What should I do with these boxes and balls?"

"Perhaps you should give them to someone who really needs them."

Punchinello turned to leave, but stopped again. "Eli?"

"Yes?"

"I don't have a place to sleep."

Eli smiled and offered, "Would you like to sleep here tonight?"

"I sure would. I'm very tired."

And so that night Punchinello slept on a bed of wood shavings. He slept well. It felt good to be in the house of his maker.